a knox

Dreams
of truth

Dreams of truth © 2023 Santana Knox

All rights reserved under the International and Pan-American Copyright Conventions. No part of this book may be reproduced or transmitted in any form or by any means, electronic or mechanical, including photocopying, recording, or by any information storage and retrieval system, without permission in writing from the publisher.

Warning: the unauthorized reproduction or distribution of this copyrighted work is illegal. Criminal copyright infringement, including infringement without monetary gain, is investigated by the FBI and is punishable by up to 5 years in prison and a fine of $250,000.

Editor: Karen Washo, Utterly Unashamed, LLC

CONTENTS

Content warning	V
1. Clara	1
2. The Warlock	5
3. Clara	9
4. The Warlock	14
5. Clara	19
6. The Warlock	32
7. Clara	37
8. The Warlock	50
9. Clara	61
10. The Warlock	70
11. Clara	74
12. The Warlock	81
13. Epilogue - The Warlock	88
About the author	91

Author Note

The content of this book is fiction. Some points are inspired by different fairy tales, while some are inspired by Indigenous Brazilian lore I grew up being told with heavy doses of my imagination added.

Content Warning

Violence, language, coercive behavior, poisoning, infertility, explicit sex.

CHAPTER ONE
-dara-

"Mirror, mirror, on the wall—Who is the most powerful sorceress of them all?" My stepmother spewed her ritualistic prayer at the enchanted mirror as she did every night since I was young enough to have memories.

The mirror tired of her question, but it never once let her know. For even Arkana knew their existence would cease if their physical forms became destroyed. Arkana were magical items, possessed with the soul of a willing creature. All Arkana were created by the Dark Wizard. They were his toys, and he was the toymaker.

There was a civil war before I was born between the people who were native to the land and the king, my grandfather. During this war the majority of Arkana were destroyed, until finally the king and the chief of the Guaraní people settled on uniting the bloodlines. My mother married the prince— my father. There were only a few Arkana left in the kingdom of Guaraní now, and only those who descended from the original inhabitants of the land could properly control an Arkana.

My ancestors.

My stepmother did not know that, and the mirror used it to its advantage.

"Mirrrror." She rolled her R's dramatically as she waited for its delayed response.

There were mage apprentices in the castle who surpassed her power. But the mirror tested and lied, always telling my stepmother, the queen, exactly what she needed to hear so that she'd leave its sight.

The problem was not that the mirror could lie.

It was that *I could not*.

I was a pariah in my own home, to my own family. The loneliness became exhausting. So after spending my eighteenth birthday alone, like I had every single day of my existence, I packed up and left. Draping the green hood over my head to disguise myself while I snuck through the palace walls and made my way out of the protected sectors.

My mother passed away during childbirth, and as it was duty of the king to provide the kingdom a male heir, he was remarried by my name day. Every child born of Guaraní blood received a blessing from the moon goddess, Jací, on their name day. Jací descended from her kingdom in the sky and took the shape of a woman to bestow her magic onto me.

What was meant to be a gift, turned out to be a curse.

"From her lips, only truth shall spill," the moon goddess told my stepmother before pulling magic from the heavens and draping it over me.

So inside the walls of this palace, I wasted away. Too important to risk going out there and not important enough to actually be regarded. They all detested my presence here, that much was clear. People thought they always wanted the truth, but the reality was that they could not handle it. And as such, they could not handle me.

I walked for hours, until the blisters on my feet were too much to bear and I knew I needed to find somewhere to rest overnight. The woods were nearby, but would they provide me shelter or expose me to something far more dangerous than the evils within the palace walls? I found a shallow cavern, just big enough for me to crouch into. It would provide me some cover against the sharp wind and the rain, but it would not do much if something wanted to make supper of me.

I took my boots off, wiggling my sore toes and rubbing the ache from my muscles. The cold was already sinking its talons into my bones. Without a fire, that was a pain that could not be remedied. I leaned my head against the stone wall and closed my eyes in hopes that I could find some rest.

I could not sleep.

The fear of waking up to a half-eaten body and the face of a creature devouring me was consuming my every thought.

Why did I do this to myself?

How could I have been so stupid to think I could have made it even one day on my own? A forgotten princess with no skills and a treacherous tongue. I was as vulnerable as a worm to a bird.

I rolled off my cape and draped it over my shoulders once more, feeling the warmth of the fur lining and receiving some comfort from it. I slipped my boots back on, deciding to venture deeper into the forest.

Within a few minutes of walking, the sky gave out and the raindrops fell. I succumbed to the fact that I was going to be soaked no matter what and instead of complaining to myself I walked forward, hoping to find shelter from the rain. That was when the small shack appeared in the distance, lodged between two dead trees.

Every part of my gut told me not to keep going, to stay as far away from the damned thing. But the cold was nearly immobilizing, and I had a feeling I was going to be facing much tougher decisions if I did not get out of the open forest soon.

CHAPTER TWO
—the warlock—

The wards that had been placed around the perimeter of the shack were wailing like banshees in the night.

There was an intruder in my forest.

It wasn't often the townspeople wandered this direction, and they seldom traveled through my woods if they did. People did not dare to end up a toy in my collection, not unintentionally at least. They had different names for me. The toymaker. The warlock.

Or my favorite, The dark wizard.

I snapped my fingers, bringing hundreds of candles to light simultaneously throughout the room and grabbing my helm off its shelf. It was ancient steel, lined with long spikes across the top, as if it were a sharp crown. The metal layered over my face, with just a slit in the middle to let the light in. Not big enough to look through. It did not matter, I would not use my eyes to see when I wore it.

I draped it over my head, feeling the magic of the Ariana coursing through my veins and multiplying my own natural power with it. I focused on the presence outside, on the boundaries where the wards had been broken. Too big to be a small animal, not vicious enough to be anything but human.

With the helm on, I could see through the walls of the shack. If I focused hard enough to tune out distractions, I could see past the trees and make out her shape.

Her shape.

Too frail and small to be a man.

How a woman made it this deep into my forest without magic to protect herself from the beasts I set amuck was beyond me. I expected to find an armored knight with a weapon, instead I found raven haired beauty drenched by the cold rain.

I reached my hand out for my cloak and it drifted through the air until it landed on my shoulders, tying itself around my neck. With a flick of my wrist the door swung out and the heavy rain poured into the shack. I stepped through the threshold, the space above me domed out from my energy, letting me stay dry as if the heavens were afraid of getting me wet.

She was frozen to the ground, paralyzed by either the fear, cold, or possibly even both. Her eyes were fixated onto the shack, so much so that she didn't notice me or my dark shadow closing in on her until it was too late.

She was a little bird of a thing, so small that I could have broken her with a hand alone and used her bones to pick at my teeth.

"P-please do not hurt me." Her teeth clinked violently from shivering.

"Who are you? How did you get this far?" I asked the girl, knowing her fear would only grow at hearing my words.

With the helm on, my voice was unmasked by my human costume. My true voice was unleashed. The voice of darkness and chaos. The voice of the eternal being that once consumed my human soul.

You were not born a dark wizard, you were made.

"Clara Nieves," she said with no resignation, a pain clouding her eyes like she was npt in control of her words. "I walked until I could no longer."

A curse. How curious.

To be cursed meant you had infuriated one of the Gods so deeply that the already insufferable existence of humanity was not enough punishment. They wanted to bleed you dry. My curiosity piqued. I needed to know the extent of her agony.

"And why did you walk this far from the village, Clara Nieves?" I asked, a visible shudder came out of her from the disembodied sound of my voice.

She bit her lip as if she was fighting back answering, her tiny fists clenched until the white of her knuckles were clear even in the dark of the night. Her nostrils flared angrily, and a bead of blood formed by her mouth before a tear slowly rolled down her cheek and she could no longer fight back.

"To find you," she blurted out with a pained cry.

"There, there Clara. Does the truth not feel as good as it should?" I placed my fingers under her chin and lifted her head up to look at me, knowing she couldn't see my face.

She shook her head, letting me know that each word she uttered was cutting away a piece of something more permanent inside of her.

Her free will.

I could help with that.

CHAPTER THREE
-clara-

I could not move.

All I could do was shake and shiver in the presence of this unsanctified abomination. His face was steel but had no eyes, was it even man? Many sharp metal horns protruded from the top of its head, or maybe it was a crown. I could not tell from below. He had to be at least seven feet tall.

"Clara." That voice was unlike anything I had ever heard before in my life.

It sent a chill down my spine and made me unwell. Pure evil. That was what it sounded like. Like all of the pain and suffering in the world had been bottled and this was the result.

"No, it does not." A tear rolled down my cheek.

He gestured towards the small shack without uttering another word. I exhaled anxiously, my teeth chattering, while I cursed myself for knowing it was this or likely death.

"What are you called?" I asked the creature.

"You know my name, little parakeet. Everyone knows my name. Everyone knows the woods belong to me," the dreadful voice spoke, shutting the door behind him with a flick of his wrist.

"You are the dark wizard, the Toymaker." I thought back to what I knew of the folklore of this place, stories told to me by my father's servants before they too had grown tired of my presence.

"And you are cursed," the voice hissed and my eyes widened.

"How did you know?" I could not hide my alarm.

"The damned see the damned," Another tear rolled down my cheek from the fear he evoked.

There was something so terrifying about this creature that I wondered if I might have preferred being eaten alive by something else out there instead. It might have been less painful. It was pure agony to cower under the presence of this *thing*.

"Then, you know what I want," I chattered out, doing my best to keep my teeth from clinking together too much.

It laughed a cold and cruel sound.

"What will you give me in return, my little parakeet?" it asked me, sending my gut into a swirling vortex of anxiety.

"Umm... I have nothing to give." I looked down shamefully.

"Do you know why they call me the toymaker?" he asked and I shook my head. "It is because I collect souls. Come out of the rain, let us strike a bargain," the voice said before returning back to the eerie shack.

It flicked its wrist at me when it noticed I had not moved yet, and as if all free will had been stripped from me, my feet grazed along the dirt, pulling me into the dilapidated home. Once inside, nothing was how I had expected it to be. It was immense. At least ten times the size that it was on the outside, and it was lavished with every luxury. It was more updated than my father's own castle. Though how it was possible I was not sure.

The floors were shiny and clean wooden planks that were stained a deep red color. Though there had only been one window from the outside, there were somehow dozens more on the inside. It was as if the outside was a lie, a mirage, something to keep others away from this place. Because it seemed as if the building I stood inside of was at least five times bigger than it appeared.

Thunder cracked through the sky, and a burst of lightning hit a nearby tree. I turned around just in time to see it split in half in a burning blaze before it fell in the forest. It made no sound, but the Earth shook below me.

He flicked his wrist again and the door swung shut behind me. Water dripped from my clothes nearly as fast as the rain fell, my fear kept me immobilized. My teeth gave me away though, chattering nonstop from both uncertainty and the cold that had made its home inside my bones.

I kept my eyes to the floor. He did not speak. The silence between us was deafening and the beating of my heart was nearly loud enough to be heard through the downpour on the other side of the windows.

"Speak," the horrible voice commanded.

"I wish to break my curse," I mustered out as bravely as I could.

It barked a laugh that sent chills down my spine. I raised my gaze up, but the steel helm was too frightening to keep my sights fixed on it. I could see clearly now the crown of steel spikes adorned its head, some were as long as my arm, some as small as my fingers. The slit in the middle provided no insight into what might lay inside. A harrowing darkness was all that could be seen. Its lack of eyes made it look more creature than human.

This was the warlock all the stories spoke of. He was the reason no one in the kingdom strayed far from the village and why no knight dared to cross the forest. He was the incarnation of evil that was reborn into our world.

"What have you done to anger the moon goddess?" he hissed out.

"N-nothing." I promised fearfully, unsure how he knew just exactly who had bestowed this 'gift' onto me.

"A princess who cannot lie," the toymaker spoke, removing its cloak from his shoulders, it floated in midair on its own.

An Arkana.

"How did you know?" I asked.

"Your curse whispers to me, begs me to wrap my hands around its neck and squeeze out every bit of lie that aches to pour from your soul." The voice fluctuated from deep to a bone chilling pitch, and at times it sounded like dozens of people spoke at once.

"What can I give you?" I asked, the helm turned, as if it were thinking curiously about my question.

Chapter Four
–the warlock–

What a fine question indeed.

I knew she was royalty from the emblems she naively wore on her wet clothing. The broch of the parakeet on her cloak had long been the symbol of the king for generations in the stolen kingdom of Guaraní.

"Remove your wet clothing," I commanded, tired of hearing her teeth clanking loudly.

I snapped my fingers commanding the hearth to fill with fire. Her hands trembled as she struggled to undo the clasps on her dress with fingers rigid from the cold. It took her far too long but the minute the dress dropped to the ground the cloak wrapped itself around her body, shielding her from me while draping her in warmth.

Curious.

Only true descendants of the original people could compel Arkana to do their bidding. She was not just a princess, she was powerful, which meant her curse was not meant to be a curse, it was just perceived this way. Gods were like that, well-meaning but with poor execution.

Exhaustive little bastards.

I was neither God, nor man. Undying but unliving.

You see, *my* curse was my forest. A long time ago I was bound to it by the thunder God himself. I drew the boundaries of my jail myself and raised the trees up from the ground. He filled it with creatures to cure my loneliness, but covered the sky with thickets of trees so that I would never see the light of day.

I preferred the shadows now, anyway.

"Stand by the fire," I ordered her.

She hobbled towards the hearth. My cloak wrapped itself too tightly around her legs not leaving her enough room to walk properly. I sat across from her, watching her nerves skyrocket with each word I *did not* say.

"Are you going to break my curse?" she asked again.

Willful little thing.

I had not quite decided if I would shatter that part of her or cultivate it.

But I *was* going to be keeping her.

"Yes," I hissed and her eyes went wide, the fear so obvious in her expression.

I would have been concerned if it were not there.

"What do you want of me in return?" she asked, for the first time really looking up and staring into the crack of my mask.

It would only show her the void, not me.

"I want you. Clara." Her eyes went wide like she did not believe me. "For a year, as part of my collection." I gestured to the wall behind me, the illusion disappearing to show the hundreds of dolls behind a glass case.

Each one contained a soul, a person who had once come to me to barter for something more. I granted their deepest desire, and eventually, when the time came, I reaped their souls and locked them away in my collection. To one day be turned into an Arkana, when the time came that they had exhausted their miserable existence.

"Me?" she asked, looking towards the shelves behind me.

I waved my hand, hiding the glass case with the illusion of the wall again and she blinked in astonished wonder.

"Yes, but fear not parakeet, I will not keep you hidden away. You will not be just a toy in my collection, but my plaything." I stood, my nearly seven foot frame towering over her before I placed my gloved finger under her chin to lift it up.

Frightened little bird.

"I shall not neglect you like the others." She did not seem reassured.

"You will break my curse if I say yes?" she asked.

"I will break your curse after the year is up," I clarified and her shoulders dropped with disappointment.

As if she thought she would somehow avoid paying up.

"But you will break the curse?" she asked again.

"I will." I stuck my hand out for the accord.

"Then I am yours," she declared, taking my hand in hers, not knowing what the words alone could do to a creature like me.

"The deal is made, princess. The only thing that can free you from me now is time. If you run from me, if you hide from me, you will pay," I warned her, she cowered, shrinking away from me. "Are you afraid?"

"Yes," she blurted out, slapping her hand over her mouth and frowning at herself.

Ah yes, how utterly satisfying. I would very much enjoy our time together. Though when you saw lifetimes of existences drifting by, a year could hardly fill the hollowness inside. I could already feel myself getting angry at the thought of our time being up when the reality was it hadn't even started.

"Bathe," I instructed, waving my hand at the ceiling, making a golden clawfoot tub drop to the ground.

I breathed heavily, attempting to reel in my anger once I saw her reaction to my outburst. I snapped my fingers, filling the tub with steaming hot water. The cloak nudged her forward and she stepped towards it, first looking back up at me. She peeled the fabric off her shoulders, letting it float in the air as she shyly stepped into the basin.

Her long dark hair fell down her back in a shiny sheet against her dark skin. Her breasts were small and her hips were full and wide. Her soul made me hungry, and I ached to possess it.

Staring at her naked body was driving me to madness. It looked soft and screamed to be touched, to be marked, to be branded by my evil. I looked away, finally breaking contact with the girl, though she couldn't see my eyes through the helm.

I saw her just fine.

"I don't recommend leaving. You were lucky once; you will not get lucky twice. Ao Ao is out there." I warned her.

"It is real?" she asked, sinking into the water with eyes full of wonder once again.

I did not answer. I disappeared through the halls, taking leave to my chambers and letting her bathe on her own. We had time to get acquainted, right now I needed to understand why this descendant of the original people was eliciting this reaction from me.

Chapter Five
-dara-

He said Ao Ao was out there and then disappeared like he had not confirmed a childhood fear of mine. Ao Ao was a terrifying beast from children's tales. Something that was told to keep the young ones in line and too afraid to rebel against their parents or commit wrongdoings.

A beast nearly six feet tall, the body of a ram, with fangs long and sharp. It stood on hind legs but it could also run on all four. There was nowhere you could hide from it, and there was no way to outrun it. I wrapped my arms around my knees and curled myself into a ball inside the tub, allowing the weight of my own decisions to fully sink in.

I left the palace.

And now I had signed myself away to the dark wizard who lived in the woods.

For an entire year.

Then I would be free.

I did not know what he could possibly want with me, but I was not stupid enough to resist such a beautiful opportunity when it knocked so loudly at my door. I would take it, consequences be damned. Soap appeared in the water with a bubbling pop sound and I lathered my skin with it before washing it away. Before I even had a chance to think about it, a towel appeared, folded, on the chair next to the tub. I stood, picked it up, and wrapped my body with it before realizing I had no idea what would come next for me.

That was when I noticed the golden footprints on the floor. I filled my lungs with air and exhaled an anxious breath, deciding to follow them into the dark hall. Looking back, with each step forward that I took, the golden path disappeared behind me.

It did not ease my anxiety, but I had gone too far to turn back. I was here for a reason, and I would do whatever it took to rid myself of this curse once and for all. To dispose of this wretched tongue that betrayed and punished me to no end and promised me a life of loneliness.

Lies were the thread that wove together the fabric of love.

That was what I had learned.

Without lies, I would never have love.

It was so dark I could hardly see my nose in front of me. As soon as I fully stepped into the hall, candles lit on their own, lining the walls and brightening what now was so clearly a very long hallway.

The footprints continued and I followed them to a closed door. Was I being guided or was I being fooled? I turned the knob, opening the door to reveal another room. A chandelier filled with candles hung above the bed, filling the space with adequate lighting. The bed was big and lavish, soft fabric draped over it luxuriously and a rug made from the hide of something dead covered the floor underneath it.

My toes curled into the fur and I took a moment to appreciate something so small yet comforting after such a harrowing day. A big vanity was next to the bed, a large mirror with a golden frame hung on the wall above the desk. There was a nightgown on the bed. I dropped the towel and slipped it over my head, before crawling into the bed and feeling myself melt into the pillow.

The land of dreams was the place I truly felt at home.

The only place where I could conjure lies and be free to speak however I wanted. No one looked at me with the familiar distaste for my cursed tongue. I was just a little girl when I realized I had more control of my dreams than I had in my real life. I honed the skill and used it to become the master of my sleep.

I painted the picture in my head, curling my toes around the soft beddings and feeling myself sink deeper into the world I was creating. I wanted bright colors, but I didn't have the same control that was normal for me. I could not be blamed, my entire world had shifted in a matter of a day.

I focused on the world I was building, grim gray trees without leaves reminiscent of the wizard's forest surrounded me. A murder of crows perched on every branch, their heads moving with every step I took.

"Caw caw." I flinched, turning my head quickly when a single bird flew past.

"You should not wander these woods alone." A smooth, deep voice reached me. "There are many beasts looking for an easy meal."

I turned, my hands slamming straight into his chest. I looked up to find the voice belonged to a handsome man, just a few years older than me. He wore dark clothing and a knight's armor over the fabric. His jaw was strong and sharp, and black hair fell down his face. He brushed it away from his eyes, revealing a piercing gray stare.

"I-I am sorry," I stammered out, realizing my hands were still pressed to him.

He chuckled, his teeth showing a pearly white grin and canines likely sharp enough to tear through flesh. As if he noticed me staring, he ran his tongue over the edges of his top teeth.

"Do not be sorry, it is my job to make sure innocent princesses like you do not get lost or eaten out here in these woods," he said, forcing heat to flood through my cheeks.

"It is your job?" I asked.

"Is that not what knights do?"

"I would not know." I shrugged.

"A princess like you is not surrounded by knights?" he asked, nothing but shameless wonder in his voice.

"No," I said, my voice cold and unfeeling.

It was the truth, and I was losing control of my dream. It was irritating me. I had not come here to be reminded of what I was running from. He seemed to have noticed.

"Well, can I escort you out of the woods?" he asked.

I shook my head.

"No, my home is in the middle of these woods." I pointed off in the distance and focused hard until a small cottage, surrounded by a meadow of flowers materialized in the gloomy, gray forest.

I painted the scenery just like watercolor on paper, the same way I could in real life. His eyes widened with surprise and he tilted his head like he meant to question it. But like a good little dream character, created for my amusement, he didn't bother. He extended his arm out to me.

"Well then, shall I escort you home, princess?" I nodded, lacing my arm through his.

Each step we took blurred as if we were taking three or four and the cottage was soon right in front of our faces. The smell of flowers was sweet in the air, as if they ignored the aura of the woods that surrounded us. The knight stood stoically, waiting for me to bring him back into the story I was carving.

"Here," I said, plucking a purple flower in the shape of a bell from the ground.

I sniffed its sweet honeysuckle-like scent before giving it to him. "For when you go to battle, it will bring you luck."

"Do you know this flower?" he asked, I shook my head. "It is Veluria. It is said to be poisonous to eat. Even the smell alone could put a grown man to sleep if breathed in too much."

"Oh!" I tossed it to the ground, heat flushing my cheeks once again, this time in shame for my ignorance. "I did not know. I promise It was not my intention." I bit my lip and he chuckled again.

"Little princess, I do not take you for the murdering by poison type." He tucked a strand of loose hair behind my ear and lifted my chin up.

I smiled, he returned it.

My stomach fluttered anxiously.

"I do not want a flower for the war, I want a kiss from you, princess." He said, making it my turn to widen my eyes in shock.

"Kiss you?" I asked.

"A flower will die, and I will mourn its death while in battle. But a kiss from you will be all I need to carry me through the war. I will think of your soft lips every day. Every sword that comes near mine will feel the hot steel of my blade crushing it down because it will be your kiss that reminds me there might be something worth fighting for."

"Then kiss me, so that you may return safely," I told him, placing each one of my hands on his shoulders and stretching onto the tips of my toes.

He was far too tall for this to be some simple feat. He lowered his neck and brought his face closer to mine, as if he was not uncomfortable by our proximity at all. I could not recall a time where anyone had been this close to me before. His kind smile was far too dashing and even though it was only a dream, it would still be my first kiss. My stomach turned anxiously, and a swarm of butterflies fluttered inside me.

Then his lips came to mine, chapped from his journey but full of need. I pressed back, feeling his hands cup the side of my face as if to urge him even closer to him somehow. Our chests touched and I clasped my hands behind his neck while his tongue parted my lips. I opened, making room and allowing him in, tongues clashing in a dance of control until a sound slipped its way from deep within my chest. A fire flooded its way down to my core, forcing me to clench my thighs instinctively as if it would provide me with some sort of relief.

He chuckled as if he could read my thoughts, lips still sealed around mine before he pulled back. He leaned his forehead against mine, letting out a deep exhale.

"Yes, I think this will help me get through the war just fine princess," he said, using his thumb to wipe the wetness from my skin around my bottom lip.

He turned on his heels as if he were going to leave but I reached out and grabbed his wrist.

"When will you be back? I do not even know your name," I told the knight.

The birds sang a loud and obnoxious tune forcing me to cover my ears and release the knight's wrist. I looked up to find the birds but could not find the little beasts. Looking back, my knight was fading into nothing. I sighed an exhale of defeat and closed my eyes, focusing on the sound of the birds and letting it connect me to the new morning.

The sun was high when I awoke, which meant it was far later than I had ever slept into the day. Dreams were like that, very little happened in what felt like such a short time, but the reality was, a thirty-minute dream took all night.

My knight was gone, and I was still in this dreary shack. The bird sang an obnoxious tune that pulled me out of my slumber once more. I sat up on the bed, throwing a pillow at the window, hoping it would scare away the annoying creature.

It did not.

I swung my legs off the bed, and once my feet touched the ground, I noticed wool lined slippers waiting for me on the floor. I slipped them on, relishing their comfort and finding a soft robe draped over a chair as well.

I walked to the door, placing my hand over the golden knob, but feeling a bit too scared to turn it myself. And then I smelled the most delicious scent. I turned back to the room, finding a small round table that I swore hadn't been there before that very moment. A platter sat on it with an assortment of different foods.

Pheasant breasts roasted golden to perfection, savory pies each bigger than my hand, turkey legs, sliced ham, fruits of every variety, and numerous styles of tarts covered the table. I was royalty, but I wasn't used to this kind of treatment. When you were used to being the pariah, you took whatever was left. You became anxious at the thought of inconveniencing anyone when you knew the moment you were gone from their sight they would be bad mouthing you to the closest person.

I asked nothing of my father's servants, and in turn, almost always ended up fending for myself. I learned to cook my meals at an early age and to mend my dresses when they became tattered. I was self-sufficient. I needed to be.

Otherwise, I wouldn't have survived.

"Clara, why is your dress torn?" Father asked.

I bit my lips to hold my answer back, but my stepmother struck my hand with a rod to keep me from holding on to the truth.

"The cook's son pushed me!" I blurted out, slapping my hand over my mouth as if it would do me any good.

Gasps were audibly heard from the servants gathered to witness by my stepmother. She was a fan of making examples of them whenever she needed to inspire better work ethics.

"It was an accident! I promise Father!" I begged before he had even had a chance to look at the boy, cowering behind his mama's dress.

He was older than me. I was a girl of eight and he was a boy of nine. We played often that year. His mother was hired as the palace head cook the previous spring and they moved into the grounds. But he was young and understood nothing of the world, and thus was bitter about their shortcomings. While playing, he asked why he slept on a straw bed with the horses while I slept inside the palace.

I told him the truth. That he was born poor and would likely die poor because the world did not make men better. It only made them keep going. He pushed me, angry and rightfully so, once the words I did not want to say were uttered.

"Fifty lashings," the queen said with a cold smirk.

The punishment wasn't truly for the boy. It was for me.

He never looked at me again after that. Never uttered a word or passed my way in the halls of the castle nor the grounds. The servants learned the lesson as well. I was not someone they could risk getting close to, despite my well-meaning.

And thus, my isolation began.

I sat at the table, grateful for the bounty in front of me. I picked up a drumstick and sank my teeth into the savory meat, letting it roll against my tongue while my teeth tore it to bits. I groaned in happiness, my belly crying out in victory with obscene sounds while I sent it food for the first time in nearly a day.

I ate my fill, only stopping every few chews to grab the chalice of wine and wash down the delicious meal. I only ate a few bites of a chocolate tart, feeling far too full to swallow anymore. I stood from the table and made my way to the door once more, this time hesitating before even reaching my hand out.

I was afraid.

Afraid of the masked wizard who lurked this magical place, even though I had willingly offered myself to him. No, I was not brave enough to cross paths with him again this soon. I took a few steps back from the door before I turned and made my way to the window instead, opening it and letting the cold breeze in. Winter would be heavy this year. I could always tell. I had a connection with the snow.

I looked back at the corner and the food had disappeared from the table. It was completely clean, like none of it had been there at all. But my stomach was full, and I wasn't going to question the dark wizard's magic. I paced the room back and forth, debating in my head whether I should step out of here or if this was going to become my own voluntary cage.

A gust cut in, filling the room with the sweet scent of fresh honeysuckle. I smiled, remembering the previous night's dream. I was feeling anxious, but the smell somehow calmed me down. I slowed my pacing and ran my fingers through my hair, taking a deep breath and filling my lungs with that calming perfume.

I had dreamt up plenty of beautiful men before. The cook's son had grown to be a fine looking man and served many warm bodies in my dreams. It was nearly impossible for your brain to create a face it had never seen before.

But my knight. Where had I seen him before?

I sat on the edge of the bed, trying to figure out the puzzle. Maybe if I knew where I had pulled him from, maybe I could get him back in the next dream. I did not like to control that many elements in my dreams, I liked to ride the wave of freedom and just paint the background picture while my heart enjoyed the story that was being told.

I yawned, stretching my arms over my head and leaning back against the pillows draped over the bed. I had eaten too much and now my gluttony was making me sluggish. I knew the feeling well from the holidays. It was the few times a year where such a surplus of food was cooked that I could fill a platter with an obscene amount of food and take it to my chambers to devour upon.

And I always ended up taking a nap after it too.

I yawned once more, deciding not to fight the feeling.

I was holding a purple flower in the shape of a bell when the dream began.

"What have I told you about those flowers, my sweet wife?" A comforting, familiar voice soothed into my ear from behind.

Strong arms wrapped around my waist pulling me closer to them. My back pressed to a firm chest, and I looked up to see familiar gray eyes and a soft smile.

Chapter Six
-the warlock-

"I cannot seem to remember," she said, twisting her head back to look up at me.

I squeezed my arms around her waist tighter and lowered my nose to the small of her neck, breathing in her scent.

She had not questioned the shift in power in the dream yet. She did not realize I had more control than her this time. Why she was asleep so soon again was beyond me though.

"I said," I whispered in her ear, feeling the skin on the back of her neck goosebump. "Those flowers are lethal, they are dangerous."

"Why do so many grow around here?" She fanned her arm out at the meadow of Veluria flowers.

"They grow where lost souls are present," I told her and her eyes grew fearful.

"Here?" She asked with a whisper-like yell.

"There are spirits everywhere dear wife." I planted a kiss on the top of her head.

"Did we marry after the war?" She was pulling pieces of the previous dream into this one.

No darling.

This was a new dream. New rules, new story.

"What war? Are you well?" I asked, giving her a dimpled half grin.

"You were not a knight before we married?" I laughed.

"I have been a farmer since I can remember my dear wife. This farm belonged to my father and now it belongs to us." I turned her to face me, using my index finger to lift her chin up so I could take a look at the beauty in front of me.

Golden brown skin and raven hair darker than the night itself. I had not intended to see her again so soon in a dream, but I could not miss the opportunity to learn more about her. Her dreams were works of art, painted with a skill that could only have been honed over time.

I kissed her, not bothering to make small talk this time as I realized the hunger was starting to become a noticeable ache. I was starving for her soul, but I would take whatever she would give me. Her hands pressed softly against my chest, and I brought a hand to her side.

"Let us go inside," I whispered, "I should like to get this dress off of you."

She bit her lip, her cheeks turning red.

"My wife does not wish to consummate our marriage? To let me fill her belly with my seed until a new life is formed there?" I watched her reaction to my testing the waters.

She exhaled a stuttered breath.

"Let us go inside then, husband." She placed her hand on my cheek and I fought back the instinctual urge to recoil, not daring to shatter the illusion and lose my control over her dream.

I picked her up, throwing her over my shoulder and forcing a yelp from her as she laughed and beat her fists against my back playfully, like this was something we had always done. Like it was something she dreamed of.

I kicked the door of the farmhouse open and walked through until we reached our bedroom. She squealed happily once I dropped her on the bed, but that squeal turned into anxious energy once I began to unbutton my shirt. I undid each one slowly, watching her eyes follow the movement of my hands with each button before slipping the shirt off my arms. She wet her lips without realizing she had done so.

She reached down to the ground, grabbing the hem of her loose gown and pulling it over her head. It was the same nightgown she had fallen asleep in, but she had not realized she did not put any attention into her clothing this time. I removed my trousers, standing bare and erect in front of her. Her eyes had difficulty looking anywhere but between my legs.

I closed in on her, pressing my body against hers and urging her to look at me. "Kiss me," I told her.

She obeyed beautifully, locking her lips around mine and parting to let me in just like she had done the previous time. She moaned, sending a bolt of energy to my engorged cock.

The kiss grew feverishly, our hands roaming each other's bodies, grabbing what we appreciated most while exploring freely. Flesh on flesh. I bit her lip playfully and she groaned again, making my already impossibly hard cock even harder.

"Are you sure you are not a knight?" she asked between heavy pants.

"If you keep thinking about it too much, you will be pulled away from me again." I pressed my erection against her belly.

I ran my hand up her side, palming her breasts and giving it a firm squeeze before flicking her nipple softly under the pad of my thumb. She moaned again, closing her eyes. I pushed her down on the bed and prowled over her. Letting one hand journey its way down the center of her legs, I blew a hot breath against her cunt as I lowered my head to admire it.

I spread her with my fingers before running my tongue down her center. She inhaled a sharp breath and cried a pathetic sound from the contact.

"More," she begged.

"Anything to please you, my dear wife." I reminded her who she was in this dream before sucking her clit into my mouth and swirling my tongue around her hot cunt like I had been eating a fine meal.

She was a damned feast, even in this dream I could taste the sweet flavor of her pussy dripping into my mouth. I ran my tongue up and down before inserting a finger inside. Her hips bucked instinctively, and I rubbed the finger against her walls, searching for the button I knew would take care of her quickly, even in a dream.

We did not have very much time.

Dreams always ended before the good part.

I inserted another finger inside, feeling her tight, velvety walls practically sucking me in and squeezing them with her vice grip. I curled them against the spot once I'd found it, thrusting in and out of her until I could see it on her face that her release was near.

"Something is happening." She ran her fingers through my black hair and pulled tightly.

Her legs shook and she screamed out in pleasure. A gush of liquid flooded from inside her, coating her thighs and my hand while she continued to buck from wave after wave of pure pleasure.

"Oh Gods!" she exclaimed. "I want to do that again." She laughed, bringing a smile to my face.

Her eyes blinked in quick flutters. I knew soon she would be awaking again. I pressed my lips to her forehead, knowing she would see me fade into nothing right in front of her eyes as reality melted into her dream before she woke up.

Chapter Seven

-dara-

I woke up to the sound of the window shutting. I was still alone in the room, but the sun was low in the sky, which meant it was nearly evening. I had slept the entire day somehow it didn't feel like it. I was groggy, unrested, and exhausted. Flashes of the dream appeared in my mind and heat spread throughout my face, I reached my hand between my legs feeling the wetness seeping out.

Food had materialized onto the table once again, but this time, there was an easel next to the window and all the supplies needed for painting. I sat, lowering it to my height and setting it up horizontally so I could use it for my watercolors. I brought the platter of food closer and began to paint the sunset while nibbling small bites here and there.

It was serene, tranquil, the most at peace I had somehow felt in my entire life, and I wasn't sure if it was because I was *here* or simply because I wasn't *there* anymore. I painted until the last rays of the sun disappeared in the horizon, capturing the beautiful world that sat just outside my window as I had learned to do at an early age. Solitude was a great companion for cultivating unnecessary skills.

I looked over my painting, doing my best to not be too critical or self-deprecating as I usually tended to be. I smiled to myself. It was an especially good one. Only there was no one to show it to. Certainly, the dark warlock didn't care about my hobbies. I was here for his entertainment, not my own. I put the paper down, deciding I'd put more work into it tomorrow once I had more light to work with again.

That was when I noticed the purple flower staring back at me. Right there on the paper I had painted, as if it was only a few feet away from my very window. The bell-shaped beauty was as vibrant as I remembered in my dreams and I had to wonder if I had really seen it out there or if my dream had been tugging at my subconscious.

Either way, painting had mentally exhausted me, providing me the stimulation I needed to now quiet my brain once again and rest. That nap had done nothing for me. As the darkness spread outside and stars filled up in the sky, I decided that it was enough for my first day as... his toy.

Whatever that meant.

The table cleared itself of food once again as soon as I finished eating my fill. The golden footprints appeared on the floor in front of me. Last time they led me to this room, following did not seem like such a terrible idea. It seemed like one thing was for certain, the dark wizard was not how I would meet my demise.

If he wanted to harm me, he could have already done so.

And he had not.

The bedroom had three doors, one was the door I had come in through, this was not where the footprints were leading me. There were two more doors, side by side on the other side of the bed and I followed the gold, wet, paint-like feet to one of them.

To my surprise it was a bathroom, and suddenly the urge to relieve myself was immense, as if I had not realized I had been holding it in all day. I also had not drank much of anything, and I knew I would need to remedy that soon. Did the wizard not realize I needed more than just food and wine to survive?

I scooped some hot water from the tub into my hands and drank it down, shuddering at the feeling of it warming my belly in the most unappealing way. I did this a few more times until I began to feel nauseous from drinking the warm liquid, but also knew It would cure my impending headache. I shrugged off the robe before pulling off the nightgown and dipping my toes into the hot water.

As soon as my body submerged, soap bubbles filled the bath with a deliciously floral scent that soothed every one of my nerves. I closed my eyes and let the water remove the ache in my still sore muscles. My journey from the castle had been an arduous one. One that I could admit was not intended for a solitary princess with nothing but the clothes on her back and a satchel of stale, dry bread.

I listened to the gentle sound of the rippling water, letting it hypnotize me into a daze. Inhaling in, letting the air fill my lungs and expand my chest before drawing it out of me slowly. I repeated the slow breaths, focusing on the light drips of water until I could hear my heart as if it were pounding outside of my chest.

"Not here, princess." The voice shook me back awake, jarring my eyes open and startling me back to an upright position.

"What?" I said out loud knowing full well I was alone and there was no one to answer me.

I stood, grabbing the robe from the ground and pulling it over my body protectively before stepping out of the tub. The footprints led me out of the bath, and I began to feel some sort of annoyance towards it. I could lead myself out of a bath just fine on my own.

But the feet took me to the second door once I exited the bathroom, and once I opened it a closet was exposed. It was a room as big as the bathroom, but filled with nothing but fine garments, clothing and dresses of all types for every occasion you could think of. Even my father, the king, had never provided me with so many.

Pity I only needed a fresh nightgown though.

I took the softest of silks off the hanger before sliding it over my head. This was a pearlescent rose-like color, and it went down to my mid thighs. No undergarments anywhere to be found.

Maybe he did not know what they were?

I snuggled into bed, pulling the heavy bedding over me and draping myself in the comforting warmth of it.

I could spend a year like this, in exchange for a lifetime of freedom from my curse. In fact, this was starting to seem better than what I had ever had before. If only it were not so lonesome here. I closed my eyes and focused on painting my dream, deciding to use my unfinished project as the inspiration.

I opened my eyes to the beautiful golden rays of the sunset painted expertly on the horizon. This was not my work, somehow it was better. I could never create such a masterpiece.

A heavy hand dropped to the top of my head before smoothing my hair down my back affectionately. I relaxed my shoulders, looking up to see the beautiful gray piercing eyes staring down at me through wisps of dark hair.

"Do you think the sun still sets if you do not watch it?" I asked him.

"At the end of the day, even for the sun, all that is left to do is sleep," the familiar voice told me, a kind expression in his eyes.

"Are you finding me or am I finding you?" I asked him, really feeling something tugging inside me that told me I had seen his face before.

I reached up to touch his cheek.

"I found you a long time ago, dear wife." He leaned into the touch; a dimpled smirk carved into his face making him twice as handsome.

I was losing my ability to push my dreams in the direction I needed them to go. Or maybe I was just expecting too much. Maybe the lesson here was to just let go and ride the waves.

"I should like to pick the flowers on the other side of the cabin, husband," I told him before taking off running through the meadow while the Sun's rays still pierced through the sky.

He chased after me, our laughter lingering in the wind like music. He caught up to me, picking me up by the waist from behind and spinning me around in circles before pulling me into his chest. He lowered his head, pressing his lips to mine softly.

I kissed him back with just as much fervor. He lost his balance, falling to the ground and bringing me with him. It was easy to laugh with him, to feel like everything was okay, that nothing hurt anymore.

He rolled us again so that I was beneath him now, his heavy weight pinning me to the ground. His knee found its way between my thighs, and he used it to spread my legs apart, making room for him there. He crawled over my body, peppering kisses down my neck and rubbing his hands up and down my sides.

I moaned and he froze.

"Let me make love to you, wife." There was something needy about his plea, like it was hurting him to have to ask me.

"Yes," I answered, knowing that when we were together, it was the least lonesome I had ever felt in my life.

His fingers worked fast, hurriedly peeling my dress off of my body. He removed his cloak, laying it on the ground for me to lay on. And then he was on me, like an animal starving for its next meal. His hands ran up my thighs and his eyes examined every inch of me, like he didn't want to miss the shape of a single freckle or forget the curve of my hips.

"Please, touch me," I begged, pulling him down to me so that I could lock my lips around his.

"Anything for you, sweet wife," his deep voice answered, sending a pool of liquid heat down my thighs.

And then two fingers were there, rubbing against my most sensitive spot, sending a current of electricity into my core and sparking me back to life. I threw my head back and moaned loudly, letting him know I appreciated his hands. That was when I felt his tongue again, doing unspeakable things to me, licking me up and down and sucking on my clit until I thought I would collapse from violent waves of pleasure.

He did not stop until I was practically crying, mewling desperately, release after release. He lifted off of me and pulled the belt off of his trousers. My vision was hazy, I was drunk with lust when his pants touched the ground. With his thick manhood in his hand he fisted himself slowly as he stood over.

For me.

"It is big." My eyes went wide.

"It might hurt," he warned me. "I do not want to hurt you."

"You will not hurt me," I reassured him. "Please."

He kneeled between my legs, placing one hand on the ground to support himself and another held him at my entrance. I squirmed, aching to feel him in some way and urging him to hurry up and do it.

It took a sharp bite of breath from my lungs when he entered me. A burning pain as he squeezed himself through my overly slick folds. I could not help crying out in pain, squeezing his flesh in my hands until my nails pierced his soft skin.

"I am not in all the way yet, you are so tight. You feel so good," he groaned, pushing himself deeper inside me. "You are doing so good." His praise sent a bolt of lightning to my belly.

He pulled out of me before pushing himself in again and going deeper than before.

"Oh," I cried out.

"Almost there, you feel so good Clara." His thumb found my clit, making circles on my still sensitive bundle of nerves and distracting me from the burn within.

"I...It hurts." It felt like I would be split apart from the inside from his engorged shaft impaling me.

"You can take me. I know you can," he coaxed gently.

He pulled out, emptying me in a sudden way that left me feeling hollow. He lowered himself back down and pressed the flat of his tongue against my center again. I whimpered. Two fingers found their way inside me, rubbing against my walls in a way that made me salivate with desire again.

"Ah," I cried at the feeling.

He thrust his fingers in and out, finding a spot inside of me that made my toes curl and the hairs on my neck stand up. I shattered around his fingers again, a pool of my arousal gathered between my legs and spilling over his cloak.

"Fuck," he whispered. "You are so wet," he groaned in my ear and with one thrust he was inside me, this time there was less pain. "You are still so tight."

He moved in and out of me slowly, as if he was doing everything he could to keep from hurting me. A vein on his temple swelled telling me this was likely one of the most difficult things he had done his entire life. The pain dulled and with every thrust he hit something deep inside of me that caused a tightening in my core, sending a burst of pleasure rippling through my soul.

"Princess, you are fucking perfect," he mumbled through grunts and groans.

"There is so much of you." I was somehow suffocating from how he felt inside of me.

"And you are taking all of it," he panted. "So good for me, princess." he coaxed, thrusting into me until I was nothing but a delirious mess of pleasure.

In and out, he moved at a deliberately slow pace, sending delicious bolts of lightning right down my center. I curled my toes and threw my head back, letting my climax shatter me until he had no choice but to follow me down into the abyss. His hot release painted my walls, filling me until I could feel him spilling out of me and just the same as the previous dreams, his image faded away as I slowly awakened.

A month came and went before I could even think about it.

It either spoke to my level of comfort in the wizard's mansion that portrayed itself as a run-down shack, or it spoke of my unhappiness in my previous life. Either way, I had fallen into a pleasing routine. I woke up to the smell of delicious foods waiting to be eaten. There were always restocked supplies for my paintings and once I had my fill of food, I'd open the window and paint.

It had become a habit, and somehow the soothing scent of the honeysuckle blowing inside always tempted me to slumber till past midafternoon. I would wake up to the window already closed, never fully rested, and continue to paint until nighttime came.

The reality was—sleep had become my newest addiction. It was the only time I got to see the man who called me wife, and somehow, I began to feel the safest around him. I knew he was just a concept of my own imagination, fabricated by my brain to help me deal with all the things I was feeling but not resolving on my own. But he was mine, created by my soul and mind and I would be keeping him until I could no longer conjure him myself.

The warlock stayed hidden, so I did as well. I felt a bitter resentment towards him. A toy in his collection for an entire year, but was I to spend them in solitude and despair all alone? Was my misery the true price to break my curse?

I dipped the brush in water before returning it to the heavy paper, adding vibrancy to the purple flower in the corner of the painting. All of my paintings were almost the same, slightly varied versions of the same image from nearly the same angle. The chair scraped across the wooden floors as I attempted to move it with one hand just a few inches to the left so that I could have slightly new scenery to capture. The trees tended to end up further away in certain paintings and in some they were much closer together as if they were somehow moving.

I knew better.

It was likely a way for my artistic gaze to not bore of its muse.

It would suffice as fresh inspiration. I could paint the inside of the room, but it was too gloomy, too grim, too dreary. Not worthy of being captured on paper. The walls were either black or green, it depended on the light, but I couldn't be too sure. Spiderwebs gathered in the corners of the high ceiling and a chandelier hung above the four-post bed.

I sighed, standing and pushing the window open for fresh air. A thought came to me.

He didn't say I could not go outside...

I gathered my easel and paint and dropped it on the grass outside the window before hiking my nightgown up my waist and stepping through it myself. I curled my toes around the soft greenery and lifted my face to feel the sun permeating my skin.

Just a few moments, then I would go back inside.

I was not planning to leave. I was not doing anything wrong.

Just a little fresh air.

I lowered myself to the ground and rolled onto my back, staring up at the beautiful clear blue sky. We were so deep in the forest, I could not believe I could see so much of it, but it seemed as if the trees were working together to make a perfect window to the heavens.

Or maybe it was the warlock's magic working here.

I rolled to my side, taking a deep breath and relishing the moment. Blades of grass tickled my fingers as I twirled them in my grasp. Then I saw it, right in front of me, as if it had been there this entire time. Maybe it had, maybe I just had not paid it enough attention.

A little bell-shaped flower, vibrant and purple just like on my paper.

I crawled over to it, curious as ever that it wasn't some figment of my dreams I kept trying to paint into existence. I lowered my face to it, taking a deep inhale. It was that same sickly sweet honeysuckle smell. I smiled, feeling that connection to my dreams that made me feel like I was in control of my life somehow.

I had no control at all.

I took another deep inhale, the scent filling up my lungs but instead of comfort it was a nauseating dizziness that had my head spinning. I laid on my back again, hoping to relieve the feeling but I couldn't catch a deep breath or clear my lungs of whatever was making me feel so weak.

My tongue felt thick, and my head was too foggy to call out for help. I closed my eyes and surrendered to sleep instead.

Chapter Eight
—the warlock—

I felt the pull to her dream.

She should not have been asleep already, but it seemed like lately it was all she did. I had never had a pet before. I was not entirely sure what she needed from me, but it seemed like she had enough to survive.

I was addicted to her, so I visited her dreams instead, letting her believe that she was the puppeteer, and I was her marionette.

Maybe I was.

THE WARLOCK 51

I found myself insatiable when it came to her. Always desperate for her presence and aching to play with her soul.

But she should not be asleep already.

I brought the helm over my head and left my quarters, stepping through the halls untill I loomed outside her door. That damned window was always open and the field of veluria nearby was constantly putting her to sleep. In small doses through the air it was not lethal, it just made humans drowsy.

She was not in the room, but the window was open.

The shell where my heart used to be throbbed with an angry pain at the thought of her attempting to escape and break her contract. But before the rage could fully settle into my bones, I looked through the walls, using my magic to see her just a few feet away, collapsed onto the ground.

I rushed outside, finding her delirious from the poison of the flower dosing her in large amounts. I had tried to tell her to stay away from it, multiple times in various dreams but she was drawn to it. It was as if somewhere deep in her subconscious she knew the flower would lull her to sleep.

I lifted her from the ground and carried her back into the shack, wondering if she was looking for me in her slumbered state. I held her in my arms and focused on seeing the image her mind conjured this time.

Slowly the shack disintegrated before my very eyes, melding into her dream as the vibrant, paint-like colors came to shape around me. We were back outside, just past her window, though

I knew this was only in her dream. She was no longer in my arms but sitting on the ground, holding the flower to her face.

"You came." She looked up at me, smiling brightly in a way that made me abandon all sense.

Then I remembered that this was a dream.

"I told you to stay away from the Veluria flowers," I scolded her, ripping the flower from her hand and throwing it on the ground.

With a motion of my hand, I wrapped my fingers into a fist, sending a powerful wave of energy from inside me to take control of her dream. The grassy meadow rotted below us, turning a sickly gray color and spreading death like a disease. Every Veluria flower died a quick death under my curse, and she frowned as she witnessed the first time I had broken character.

"What did you do? How did you do that?" She looked around with confusion.

"You could have gotten hurt. You could have died." I continued to scold her, ignoring her questions. "I told you to stay away."

"I-I just wanted to see you. I'm all alone when you are not around." Tears welled in her eyes, letting me know that truth was not her curse.

It was solitude.

"You knew what would happen?" I asked her, lifting her up from the ground and cradling her in my arms.

She nodded her head, a tear rolling loosely down her cheek. I caught it with the back of my index finger and wiped it away.

"You are not a part of my dreams, are you?" she asked, though I knew she already knew the answer for herself.

"No, parakeet," I confessed. "But I thought you would feel more at ease if you saw me how you wanted to. As a knight, a protector, a lover. Someone you could trust."

"How can I trust you if you deceive me?" she asked, something like anger flashing across her face.

"You think it unfair that I can create illusions while you're not even able to utter a single one?" She turned her head to the side as if she refused to acknowledge where the root of her feelings came from.

It was as if she refused to answer because she'd grown so used to the truth that she had forgotten that her dreams were the only place she was free to lie.

"Then I will not lie to you Clara," I vowed. "For as long as you belong to me, only truth shall spill from my lips." I waved my hands again, removing us from her dream and letting the paint melt around us, a psychedelic kaleidoscope of colors fusing into one another until all that was left was the shack once again.

I was still standing there, in the center of the room, holding her in my arms. With a stuttered soft breath, she inhaled and fluttered her eyes open. In her sleepy-like state she yawned, looking around before her eyes focused on me.

On the helm.

Her expression turned fearful, and she jumped from my arms, falling on the floor and scampering backwards like prey ran from its predator.

"It was you all along?" she asked, feeling betrayed.

"Are you upset that you did not dream me up, or are you upset that I invaded your dreams? Or is it that I was exactly what you had been looking for all along, princess?" I asked the sound of my voice morphing from the dream into the disembodied voice that came out so naturally from the helm.

"I am upset because I cared for you, and it was just a game to you."

"Is that what you truly think?" I stepped closer, towering over her and encroaching her in my shadow.

"You said I was here for your amusement." Her eyes lowered as if filled with shame.

"And you think this is me playing with you?" I asked her, pulling her chin up so I could see her eyes when she gave me the truth.

"Yes," she whispered out.

I let out a dark chuckle.

"Not yet, parakeet. *Do* you want me to play with you?" I asked.

"Y-yes," she stammered out nervously before biting her lip to hold something more back.

"Say it," I commanded her.

She took a slow, calculated step towards me, nearly closing the distance between us. She tilted her chin up high to look at me and asked, "Are you man under there?"

I did not answer.

She took one more step, placing her hands on my robes over my chest. She breathed heavily, her eyes going everywhere all at once as if she weren't sure where to focus her attention.

"Would you like to find out?" I asked and she jerked her head back up, her eyes wide with curiosity before she nodded.

I grabbed her wrist and squeezed tight through gloved hands, forcing a pained whimper from her lips. I slipped her hand through the layers of fabric until the soft palm of her hand made contact with my flesh. Her hand on my heart, each thump strong enough to push her fingertips away.

"You are warm." She sounded surprised, running the tips of her fingers over my chest.

I exhaled a sound that sounded more beast than man, not remembering the last time I'd been touched by anyone. Not in this lifetime at least.

"Do not start something you cannot handle, princess. I will take you if you entice me," I warned her, wondering if it would be fear or arousal that I would find between her legs right now.

She was not looking at the face of the knight in her dreams. She was seeing the steel, faceless helm with a crown of spikes on its head. She was seeing the embodiment of darkness, of magic tainted by the gods themselves. If it did not strike fear in her very soul, I would have thought something was wrong with her.

She did not pull her hand away, instead she created a path south, gently tracking her way to where my cock throbbed and ached for her touch. The part of me that craved for a soul to still reside within the shell of my body wanted nothing more than to make love to the beautiful woman in front of me. The part of me that knew that soul was long dead wanted to bend her over and mercilessly fuck her until she shook and quivered at the feeling of my dick splitting her open.

"Clara," I warned her, seeing the hairs on her arm come to stand from the sound of my voice.

She continued to trail her fingers lower, skin on skin until her hand found my shaft, hard and thick at just the thought of her touch. I reached behind her head and grasped a fistful of her hair in my hands. I pulled tight, earning a wince from her.

"Out here. I am not the knight from your dreams," I hissed menacingly.

"If you wanted to hurt me, you would have already." She looked up at the helm before wrapping her fist around my cock and squeezing tight.

Knowing it was nothing but the truth almost made it worse. I released her hair and instead I moved my hands to the back of her neck before squeezing. She narrowed her eyes at me like a challenge and moved her hand up and down my entire length.

"No one is here to save you." I gave her one final warning.

"I do not need a knight."

"We will see about that, princess." I would not turn her away.

I tightened my grip around her neck and forced her onto her knees. I dropped my robes to the ground and stepped out of my clothing. My cock sprung free inches from her face, her eyes burning brightly at the sight of it.

"My sweet little parakeet. Did you miss the way I felt between your legs?" she nodded. "And now you want to know what the real thing is like?"

"Yes." She looked up at my cock, wetting her lips instinctively.

"Open your mouth." She obeyed, wrapping her lips around her teeth the same way I had taught her in her dreams.

She relaxed her throat, taking me in and swirling her tongue around my full length as I pulled in and out of her mouth. She took ragged breaths when she could afford to, but I only sped up my rhythm, thrusting myself as far back as I could until I almost bottomed out inside her. Tears rolled down her cheeks, wetting her face but she moaned in response to every slam of my hips.

I did not want to finish in her mouth, I wanted to finish in her tight hot cunt while it suffocated my cock to death. I stepped back, taking each glove off my hands before pulling her up from her knees.

"Are you wet for me Clara?" I wondered what the fear the helm naturally invoked was doing to her.

"Yes." She gave me the truth.

"Show me," I commanded her and she pulled her nightgown up, raising it above her thighs and dipping her fingers between her legs.

I had given her every style dress she could have imagined, things even her father the king would not have been able to pay for himself. Instead she wore these nightgowns day in and out.

She drew herself out, showing me the sticky arousal dripping from her fingers.

"Lick it clean," I told her again, her eyes widened in horror. "Now."

She obeyed, shoving both fingers in her mouth and closing her eyes like she felt shame while she savored the taste of her own cunt.

I pulled at the nightgown, tearing it in half and peeling it off her shoulders, leaving her bare and exposed to me. She did not shy away or cover herself. She knew that I desired her, I had proven it already.

I grabbed her thigh and wrapped her leg around my hip, with my free hand I caressed her clit, rubbing circles and moving up and down until her nails dug deep into my flesh with a piercing pressure.

Shaking in my hold, she dropped her head forward, leaning it on my chest and whimpering out her climax pitifully. I wrapped my arms around her waist and carried her through the shack until we were at her bedroom door, kicking it open and dropping her to the bed.

"Take the helm off." She tried to pull me down to her but instead I brought her to my lap, straddling her over me.

"No," I answered.

"I want to kiss you," she pleaded, pausing before arching her eyebrows seductively. "Husband." She reminded me she vividly remembered my deceitful ways.

Most people did not remember their dreams, the fact she had so much control of hers and could still remember them when waking was not a surprise to me though. She was of the original people and lucid dreaming was a skill well possessed within their bloodlines.

I did not answer, instead I lined the tip of my cock to her entrance, dripping with arousal and proof of her orgasm. I rubbed the swollen head up and down her slit, and she writhed against me, moaning in anticipation. I gripped her hips, digging my fingers into her soft flesh before sinking her down into my cock.

"Ahh," she cried out from pain but I was not even halfway inside her yet.

"You wanted this," I reminded her, pulling her chin up and forcing her to look at the steel faceless thing she had let inside of her. "You still want it?"

"Yes," with her answer I plunged all the way in, sheathing the full length of my cock inside of her.

She squirmed and whimpered, squeezing my forearms from the discomfort of the sheer size of my cock piercing through her. I reached down, feeling the sticky mixture of her arousal and blood seeping between us and gathering it in my fingers to rub her clit with.

It took all of my self-control to not come inside her immediately, so I savored this chance to make her come once more just from the friction my fingers provided that swollen little rosebud. She was so fucking tight and with every bolt of pleasure I forced out from her she clenched tighter, nearly forcing me to lose it.

She came again for me, milking my cock with cries of ecstasy and a dazed look on her face that let me know her lust was beginning to take control here.

"More," she moaned.

I cupped her ass cheeks and moved her up, lifting her off my cock almost completely before thrusting back up to fill her in one movement.

"Please," she cried again circling her hips while she chased wave after wave of pleasure I doled out.

I held her hips, moving her to the tempo I desired and using her cunt for myself. I knew that with each time I skewered myself deep inside her that she was that much closer to going over the edge again. She clenched her walls around me again, shattering in my hold and squeezing my cock until I had no choice but to follow her into oblivion.

I slammed my hips one final time, emptying my release inside her before pulling out and watching it seep out from her. I pushed it back inside before laying her on her back and hovering over her.

"Just imagine, you full of my cum until you have no choice but to grow my baby in your belly. Then you would be mine forever, parakeet." I said the words, immediately regretting showing my true desires.

The one thing I could never have.

My vulnerability.

CHAPTER NINE
-dara-

I was sore, but in the kind of way that only filled me up with heat when I thought about it. We had barely just finished but yet just closing my eyes and thinking of him pushing his release back inside of me made me bite my lips and try to hide the flush that burst through my cheeks.

His baby.

He said it as if it was meant to be a threat. Like he' would be trapping me into staying longer than the year. He did not realize that it was already my deepest wish. Now that I knew it was him in all of my dreams, that I had not been alone all this time but in his company. It comforted something inside me.

My hand instinctively hovered over my bare belly at the thought of his words.

"Are you thinking about it?" the disembodied voice asked.

It was killing me to not see his face. Try as I could, I was only able to see it in my dreams, a flash of a gray eye here or there in my memory but never a full picture.

"Yes." The truth forced its way out of me before I could seal my lips shut.

"No one stays, parakeet. They all leave when they get their hearts desire," he told me through the steel mask.

"Without their souls?" I remember the wall filled with wooden dolls.

"A barter is a barter."

"And you will let me leave with mine?" I ask him.

"A year from now!" he shouted as if I had angered him by reminding him, raising himself off of me and draping himself in his dark robes once more.

I pulled my torn nightgown from the ground and brought it up to my chest to cover me while he paced back and forth in front of me.

"In my dreams... are you pretending to be kind to me?" I asked and he stopped in his tracks.

"I am kind *because* they are your dreams. Step into my mind and you would not survive a minute princess. I will trade a dream of yours for a few nightmares of mine. I will show you where death resides." His helm was a fraction of an inch away from my face and I contained my fear as best as I could.

Not that I needed to.

He knew exactly what it did to me.

And what it did to me was sliding between my thighs once again in liquid pools of heat.

"I have work to be done, princess. Is there anything you require?" He backed away, standing upright once more at his full height.

"You have left me alone in that room." I rubbed the sides of my arms anxiously. "I would like to walk freely in the woods. We had an agreement. I will not be leaving."

"You may wander within reason. I will not sacrifice the creatures in this forest to protect you from them if you stray from within the safety of my magical boundaries." I warned her and she nodded, accepting my terms.

"I should like to take a walk, then." I told him.

"Return by nightfall," he said, waving his hand at me using magic to dress me in a black dress, the corset snuggly tied perfectly in place.

Seeming content, he turned and waved his hand at the wall. The illusion shattered, revealing the shelves filled with tiny wooden dolls of all shapes and sizes. He took a moment to look them over before picking out one dressed in suspenders and threw it on my lap.

"What is this?" I asked.

"Pinocchio. Take him wherever you go." He flicked his wrist and the doll before me grew four times in size and took the shape of a human.

"Watch over her," the sinister voice instructed the doll. "And I shall free your soul and return it to its original body," the dark wizard promised.

It was an odd thing, clearly more toy than man but if you looked into its eyes there was no doubt inside it was a true soul.

"Go," The Dark Wizard commanded, flicking his wrist in command and the cloak flew off the wall, tying itself around my neck and draping me in warmth.

The thing he called Pinocchio took orders to heart. Grasping my hand and leading me out of the shack. I turned my head, looking back to see the wizard heading deeper into the halls.

"If you plan to run away, you must take me with you. If I come back without you, I might as well end myself." The wooden, humanoid like creature spoke, still holding my hand.

He was my size, and though he felt human to the touch, from his appearance he looked very much like a wooden doll.

"I am not running away." I took the lead walking away from the cabin and through the trees. "Why does he have you?" I asked.

He looked back at me fearfully, like he wasn't sure if he could trust me with his story.

"My daughter was sick, so I brought her into the woods and found the warlock like the village gossip had promised. He agreed to cure her, for my soul. At first I thought it preposterous, but in the end a parent's duty is to ensure the best for their child, is it not?"

It felt as if my heart was being crushed inside a heavy fist.

"He stole your soul?" I asked, looking into his bright brown eyes.

"No." He shook his head. "I gave it, and I would do it over and over again knowing she is out there, healthy and living."

"You are a good father," I told him, walking up the hill towards a moraberry bush. "What does he do with your souls?" I asked him.

"You do not know?" he asked, and I shook my head. "The Arkana." He pointed at the magical cloak that draped over my back.

I frowned, shaking my head in disbelief and focusing on the bush full of delicious purple berries. Maybe I should not be listening to a wooden man. I did not ask him anymore questions and he seemed content to stand by in silence while I enjoyed my time outdoors. I held the edges of my dress in my hand, creating a basket for the berries I picked, deciding not to eat them all straight from the bush.

"M-My lady," Pinocchio chirped nervously behind me.

"Yes?" I turned my head to see him pointing a few feet in the distance.

A creature stood on its hind legs, the body of a ram and canines sharp and long. The Ao Ao. It dropped to all four and stepped slowly, one foot in front of the other until it was directly in front of me. I opened my hand, revealing some moraberries for the creature to eat.

It sniffed at my hand before licking the berries up in one try. I reached out, caressing its furry human face. Its expression turned soft and it leaned into my touch, stepping even closer to me. We stood like this for a while, the creature and I, enjoying each other's company and comfort as if we were both hypnotized by some sort of spell.

I heard the ruffling of leaves, but it was Ao Ao who turned its head first. I followed the path of its eyes to three soldiers not too far in the distance. Not just any soldiers, the queen's soldiers. The creature peeled its upper lip up and began to snarl at the soldiers who were still oblivious to our presence as they continued to approach us.

The creature barked a wretched sound and the soldiers halted.

"Princess?" one of them asked, it was the cook's son.

His face was unchanged in my memory, though he had a rugged beard now.

"The queen would like to know of your whereabouts, my lady." The soldier next to him spoke and Ao Ao snarled in warning.

"I am here of my own accord, it is of no matter to the queen. Turn back now!" I told them, not hiding the anger in my voice and Ao Ao recognized it as well.

It sent the creature into a frenzy, descending down upon the soldier and attacking them with its sharp claws and teeth as long as fingers. The soldiers ran but the creature chased them down on all fours, disappearing into the thick darkness of the forest.

"We should go, milady, before the wizard worries." Pinnochio snapped me out of the daze, grabbing my hand once again.

We followed the path back to the grim shack, and that was when I realized how quickly it had become home.

Once I returned, the wizard locked Pinochio back up on the shelf, despite my complaints that he was not fulfilling his promise. The dark wizard said he told the doll to watch over me, and that contract would only be complete once my year was up as well. The doll seemed to understand better than I could have, so I let it go, not making a bigger fuss over it than I needed to.

He hung the timeline over my head like he could not wait to get rid of me and it was confusing to no end. I told him of the soldiers in the forest and though at first he seemed angry and contemplated heading out there himself, in the end he seemed to feel sure that the Ao Ao would have gotten to them before they could escape the forest.

The months quickly went by in the mysterious shack, though every day felt much more fulfilling than the last. I painted a few hours a day and took long walks through the woods with my toy-like companion. The ram creature joined me nearly every time and seemed content with my presence regardless of whether I had any food for it or not. I felt safer around it than I ever had in the palace walls, surrounded by my father's men.

A few times I had been able to find the wizard outside of his quarters, and with every ounce of confidence I could muster, I would seduce him into taking my body for his pleasure, as well as my own. He still visited me in my dreams, but because I wasn't able to see him as much as I craved since he had gotten rid of all of the bell shaped purple flowers in the area, I still felt lonely. He was not living up to his promise, maybe because he didn't know how to.

I had a feeling that the helm had something to do with it. In my dreams he was always free to be whoever and however he wanted to be. With the helm on, it seemed like he was left with no choice but being this king of darkness.

I stood outside the shack, watering the flowers that were now growing there. Ao Ao lingered by, eating grass but always vigilant. I looked up from my pail of water and suddenly she was there. Old and wrinkled pale skin stretched over her bones, her back hunched as she walked and her cane dug into the dirt with each step she took. A gray cloak draped over her back and as she stepped closer the creature snarled at her.

She froze.

"I mean no harm child," She smiled a sickly display with missing teeth and the ones that remained were rotted and brown.

"What do you want?" I asked the old woman.

"Why, to help you. I was called by the unfulfilled heart's desire," she explained. "What is it *you* want, child?"

"I want. I want." I took a moment to think of the right words. "I want the wizard to want to keep me," I told the old woman.

"That is an easy one, you just need a baby. An heir. No man will turn away their child and make them a bastard." Her voice was slimy and full of mischief, but her words spoke nothing but the truth.

He had said it himself. I would get to stay forever if I carried his child.

She reached into her cloak and pulled out a bag of apple seeds, pouring a few into her hand before turning it over onto mine. "Eat these, hurry child. Eat them now. The baby will grow in your belly and the wizard will keep you for all time."

"Are you sure?" I asked her and she pushed my hand towards my mouth.

I ate the seeds, chewing them and scowling at their astringent taste. Before I could ask how the magic would work, my head began to spin and my breathing became shallow and labored. I dropped to the ground and my extremities turned cold. I attempted to speak, to scream, to cry for help, but I could not. Nothing worked, nothing moved, nothing could be done. The witch hobbled away, cane pressing to the ground but in the distance she shapeshifted into the form of an elegant, tall woman.

Chapter Ten

-the warlock-

I heard the beast causing a ruckus in the garden. It was protective of her. In all my time in the forest, I had never seen that beast be anything but hostile to anyone and anything it encountered. But it had taken to Clara, and it had decided she was worth guarding. Ao Ao were fierce protectors, and if anything, it just kept my mind at ease when they were out there together.

The fact he would not settle down let me know something was far too wrong. I slipped the helm over my face and rushed out of the shack, finding her laying on the ground unconscious.

I had gotten rid of every Veluria flower within a five-mile radius, and it was not an easy feat. Those little beasts were invasive as hell and where one was plucked a hundred more grew in its stead.

It took a lot of magic to cast a spell strong enough to keep them from growing. So I knew this was not the flower's poison. Something else was wrong. The Ao Ao hissed and snarled, baring its teeth at me while circling around her like it was unsure if it wanted me to get close to her.

"Calm yourself," I warned the beast, raising my finger in the air.

It sat on the ground next to Clara, her skin was a sickly pale color like all the life had been drained from her. There was something taking root inside of her, killing her from the inside out.

I brought her inside, wielding my magic to raise a stone from the ground and shape it into a bed that would hold her size in the center of the shack. The beast followed inside and I didn't bother to turn it away. Caring for something human had proven to be the most exhausting task of my entire existence.

Fragile little things, always coming far too close to death at every chance they got. Almost as if their entire livelihoods centered around the fact they would one day be gone, and so they catapulted towards their demise in order to get there faster to dull the pain of it all.

I called to the magic that kept her under, commanding it to release her to me and leave her body. But it was strong magic.

The kind of magic built from generations of hatred and deep coveting. The kind of magic that could only be broken with an act of true love.

How utterly cliché.

I tried to reach her subconscious, but wherever she was trapped, she was not dreaming. She was ceasing to exist. She was dying.

And I was not the knight she needed to rescue her, I was the villain, and my hope all along had been to damn her to me, not free her soul. I was draining my own magic out of my body, pouring every bit of myself into her with the hopes that it would cure whatever was ruining her.

It was no use. The helm kept most of my power from going to her, its own purpose was to make sure my magic was amplified for myself but not to harm others.

There was only one way through it. To save her, I would be cursing her to me for all time. Because to save her meant removing the helm, and by removing the helm and seeing my face, she would no longer be human either.

That was the true reality of my curse. Unmeasurable, unending power and lifetimes with no one to share it with but the souls I had collected in my miserable time walking this earth.

In the end, our curse was the same.

Her chest moved slower and slower, her breathing growing more shallow and labored by the second. I was running out of time.

I removed the helm, dropping the heavy steel to the floor with a loud clang before focusing back on the princess laying on the stone slab. All of us were just toys, puppets for the amusement of Gods, and her fate was no less. She deserved more than an endless lifetime with me in this forsaken forest. But it was all that I could offer.

I pressed my lips to hers, relishing the soft feeling of lips that I had only known through foggy dreams lost in my memories. In that kiss, I poured every ounce of magic in my body and channeled it into hers, until her skin began to glow and her eyelids fluttered open. She choked on something and began to cough until seeds spilled out of her mouth. She looked up at me in horror, eyes wide while she began to piece together what happened.

Chapter Eleven
-dara-

He stood there clear as day in front of me.

There was no doubt in my mind it was the knight from my dreams. The piercing gray eyes and the tragically beautiful face was seared into my memory but locked somewhere tight where I could only access it during my sleep. But there he was, standing above me with a pained look on his face, eyebrows furrowed and nostrils flared like I was the cause of that anguish.

"It is you. It is really you. You saved me again." I brought myself to an upright seated position with his help.

He looked down to the ground and my eyes took notice of the helm, it looked the same as it always had but for some reason it did not strike the kind of fear into my soul that it did before.

"I did not save you," he said, voice laced with regret.

"I am alive because of you. The witch poisoned me—" I said but he interrupted.

"That was no common witch, this kind of poison magic is only known to the royalty of the eastern lands. I had only one choice when it came to reversing it, princess. It was this or your death," he explained, but I could only focus on the first part of what he said.

"My stepmother was a princess of the eastern lands." He gave me a look that condemned her. "Why would she have done this? I posed no threat to her, I practically banished myself from the kingdom." My eyes flooded and threatened to spill with tears.

"Because you hold more power, more hope, more truth, more beauty than she ever could, parakeet. And that is something to be feared by all." He wiped a tear that rolled its way down my cheek.

"You are beautiful," I whispered.

"Did you hear what I said, princess? I did not save you."

"Yes, you did. I was lost in the darkness, and you pulled me out."

"I removed your curse only to gift you with another." His voice was deep and soothing, still familiar from my dreams.

"What do you mean?" I asked him.

"In order to save your life, I had to transfer some of the source of my own power into your body." He ran his fingers through his dark hair with a frustrated sigh.

"That doesn't sound like a curse, that sounds like you saved me." I reached for him, but he stepped back, shaking his head.

"You do not understand, I took the choice away from you. I was going to give you the choice to leave. Now, now it is too late."

"What choice? What did you do?" I asked, trying to make sense of his half explanations.

"The essence of my power now runs through your veins, it is what keeps you alive now. It is as much a part of you now as it is a part of me. And because of that we are now connected; bound together through magic. Physically inseparable due to the chains that link my magic to you, keeping you alive." He narrowed his eyes, waiting for my response.

I blinked slowly, shifting my gaze to the ground while I took in the weight of his words.

"Clara..."

"You thought death would be a better fate than being bound to you for eternity?" I asked him, finally looking back up into those bright gray pools. "I ate those seeds because she made me believe you'd keep me if I gave you a child."

"I am not a being who can create life, Clara. I cannot have children. And now, neither can you. She will pay for what she has done." His voice turned cold and sinister, his gaze shifting back to the helm.

"She can wait," I breathed out, reaching for him.

I thought I would feel sad at the idea of not becoming a mother, but the reality was that I did not feel anything at all about it. I could not lament something that I had never truly wished for, especially when I had only wanted it because I thought it would bring me closer to him.

Now I had him.

I did not need anything else.

His eyes warmed with a hunger I could only faintly remember in my dreams.

"What is it you want?" he asked me, a mischievous look in his eyes that suited him more than I could have ever imagined.

"I want you to call me your wife." I pressed my lips against his.

He pushed his tongue into my mouth, and I moaned, desperate to feel his touch as my heart overflowed with the consuming thought that we would never be apart. It was just me and him, for all eternity. He broke the kiss, giving me a gorgeous, dimpled smile.

"Anything for you, wife," he teased, moving south and dropping his head between my legs.

I exhaled in anticipation, the feeling of his hot breath against my most intimate parts was enough to make me want to explode. But it was the feeling of his tongue raking against my swollen rosebud and making circles over and over until I thought I would go hoarse from crying out in ecstasy.

I came fast, squeezing his head between my thighs while his fingers pumped slow, methodical strokes in and out of me.

"Oh, Gods!"

He ripped through his robes before undressing me fully and pulling me off the stone slab. He wrapped his fingers around my throat and pulled me close to him, his jaw clenched tightly, and he spoke through gritted teeth.

"You wanted to stay, of your own accord?" he asked in disbelief.

"Have I dreamt of anywhere else?" I answered with my own question.

His face twisted up in deep thought while he analyzed every dream of mine he had visited. He looked like he wanted to believe me but there was something deep inside of him that maybe did not know how to. And that was when I realized I had answered him with a question, without a truth, for the first time in my life.

"You broke my curse." His fingers squeezed my neck as if the truth did not please him any longer.

"My magic fixed every curse, every ailment, every scratch on your body that did not mean you well." His words caused me to swallow hard against the weight of his hand.

"You say that like it is a bad thing," I scratched out.

"Being bound to my side for an eternity, is a far greater curse than the truth, princess," he sneered, putting his intolerance for himself on display.

"It is a choice I would have made for myself," I told him, pushing my body closer to his and watching his face change.

"You will never be free, parakeet. Your soul is caged inside mine now. You will always hunger for me, you will always crave me, and your loneliness will only be cured by my presence. If I die, you will die and the same for me as well." He said menacingly, loosening his grip as if to show remorse for taking that choice from me.

"Good," I whispered, bringings his hand back up to my throat and narrowing my eyes seductively.

He chuckled darkly. But what he did not know was that I was already feeling that hunger. I felt it from the moment I first walked into this shack, even when his face was hidden by the frightening helm.

"We will see about that."

He flipped me around and brought his hand between my shoulder blades, pushing my chest down to the slab and bending me over it. He pulled at my hips, and I turned my face to the side to look back at him. He stood behind me, the thick hard steel of his length pressed to my entrance as if he was waiting for my permission.

"Please," I begged. "I need you."

In one thrust he was inside of me, filling me up completely until my jaw went slack and my speech was gone. Like pouring gasoline on a fire, it was satisfying, destructive, and all consuming.

"You are so good at taking my cock, princess. That tight little pussy has never felt good for anyone else, only me," he whispered. "Say it."

"Only you. Only you," I mumbled unintelligently through rough strokes that pushed me harder and harder against the stone bed.

His hands wandered between my legs until his fingers unerringly found my clit, rubbing precise circles until my head felt dizzy and my core tightened with a need to explode and unravel all around him.

"Oh, Gods!" I cried out as a frenzied wave of pleasure burst through my body.

As if the sound pushed him further into madness, he thrusted harder and faster than before, chasing his release until I could feel him emptying himself inside of me with one final thrust and groan. He collapsed over me, breathing hard labored breaths until his hands found my breasts beneath me and squeezed.

He pulled me up with him, my back stuck to his chest from sweat but neither of us caring to separate from each other. We had each other three more times, the unsatisfying hunger he spoke of so clearly apparent to me now.

And we had an unending lifetime of it. To be in love and always craving one another.

True fairytale bliss.

CHAPTER TWELVE
-the warlock-

"What do you desire for Clara?" I asked her as she lay naked and spent on my bed now.

"Aside from revenge, I am fulfilled," she chuckled out softly.

We sat in the center of the shack and she leaned into me, resting her head against my chest with her chin tilted up so she could look upon my face.

"What is it?" I asked her, running my fingers over her soft flesh and feeling it pebble under my touch.

"You really are beautiful. Why did you cover your face with the mask for so long?" She reached up to caress my cheek, I leaned into the unexpected comfort of her warmth.

"My power is wild, abrasive. Only the helm can contain it. The beasts in this forest have all been touched by my power and felt its corruption. They are unending, just as I am, just as you are now. We belong to the forest, for anyone not born from the original people of this land will decay at sight of my magic."

"What? Why?" she asked, confusion written all over her face.

"A long time ago, the thunder God meant to use me as a weapon of extermination. He stood aside, not interfering in the intricacies of humanity while boat after boat filled with strange men declaring they were discovering new lands landed on Guaraní's shores. They mercilessly slaughtered the thunder God's children, but it was far too late by the time Tupã took notice," I explained, watching her expression change as she listened intently to the history of her people.

Of my people.

With a deep exhale I continued.

"He found me on the battlefield, trampled, bloody, and dying. He granted me immortality and commanded me to rise to my feet. He filled my weak body with his power and stated I would be free of his death once the land was cleansed of the filth that washed itself ashore."

"But you did not do it?" she asked, knowing damn well how history played itself out.

"Soldiers dropped to the ground, decaying into nothing but bone before my very eyes. Though I am still in that body I was just a young man then, I knew nothing of the world. I told him I was not his to use and to let me die, thinking that would be the end of it. I thought I would be no better than the men who raped and pillaged a land they were strangers to, if I fulfilled the task given to me.

I refused to believe I was meant to be a weapon of death. I regret my innocence now. However, it was the thunder God who was weak and shameful for using me instead of asserting his power on his own. Instead, he laughed at my suffering and told me it was a just punishment for not carrying out his orders. He disappeared, leaving me in the trenches of death. I raised the trees up from the ground myself once I learned their foliage helped absorb and deflect some of that raw power and turn it into energy. So I surrounded myself with them, to protect everyone else from me. The trees, they created the very forest we stand in now, princess."

"Who frees you from *your* curse if the thunder God is gone?" she asked innocently.

"It is your curse now too, Clara."

"A curse would keep me away, not bring me closer to you," she explained in a matter-of-fact way that I could not find an argument for.

"And what will you do, now that you have me close to you, parakeet?" I asked.

"I will use you as *my* weapon," she said as if she knew the power she held over me.

"Kill the queen?" I asked and she nodded her head, her eyes hardening.

I stood and with a flick of a finger I dressed her in a fine black gown. From the earth I pulled out an iron ore with ease. I infused heat into it as it floated in midair in front of our very eyes, taking shape of a smaller helm.

One meant for her.

It glowed a bright red color and her eyes sparkled its reflection back to me. With a few more waves of my hand the ore finalized its welding, taking on the appearance of the helm. I dropped to the ground with a heavy clang and she ran to reach for it.

I stuck my arm out to stop her.

"Do not touch it, it's hot," I warned, snapping my fingers and dressing her in armor. "Just in case," I whispered in her ear.

"I thought I was immortal?" she asked.

"Pain however, still very much exists." I dressed myself in armor before picking up her helm and carrying it under my arm.

I waved my wrist at the shelf and Pinochio descended, materializing into something reminiscent of human.

"It has been 225 years since you came to me, your daughter is long dead. Shall I free your soul, or will you join a higher purpose?" I asked and his eyes glanced at the new helm and then the princess.

"I am ready, Toymaker. I will keep the princess safe," the doll agreed, allowing me to fuse it to the helm, providing it with the true power it needed to become an effective Arkana.

"Is he gone?" Her face was the picture of sadness, and maybe I should have explained to her the process before merging the doll's soul with the helm, but had I told her she would have likely not allowed me to go through with it.

Pinochio knew this option freed him, but it also freed her too.

She followed me out of the house where the Ao Ao was waiting for us.

Or rather, for her.

"Do you think she has already made it back to the kingdom?" she asked me, a hopeless look in her eyes.

"No, I think it will be a few days before the trees let her out," I said with a smirk, forgetting she could no longer see my face.

"The trees move?" she said, the shock evident in her eyes.

"It is the only way to keep the humans from mapping it out, from being able to learn to navigate through here."

"It makes sense. I thought that the trees were moving outside my window, but I could not believe it, I thought maybe my eyes were mistaken. That maybe I had lost the angle."

"They are sneaky bastards," I told her, feeling the helm cooled down before handing it to her. "Put it on princess."

"I am not a princess anymore," she said before slipping it over her head. "I am your wife." She spoke with a sinister voice split apart by a thousand suffering souls.

My cock hardened, straining against the pants that were contained by the shell of the armor. I pressed the palm of my hand to a tree, sending my energy into it and sending out the command through the forest.

In the distance a scream could be heard. Clara's head whipped back to look at me.

"That was her?" she asked.

"She will stay preoccupied until we get to her," I assured her, taking her hand and making our way through the woods.

A path cleared out in front of us, leading us exactly where we needed to be. The Ao Ao took off running in front of us, growling and barking defensively. It took only a few minutes for us to arrive. She hung in midair, arms bound by vines and branches that kept her suspended between two trees.

"Release me!" the old witch screamed.

It was hard to tell if this form was the disguise or her true shape.

"This is where you die, stepmother." Clara spoke like the true queen she was, even if all she'd ever rule over would be me.

"Clara, stop this nonsense," she tried to command as if she was the one with any control over the situation.

The vines tightened around her wrists, and she howled painfully.

"You could have left me alone, but you just couldn't let me be could you? Did the mirror finally tell you the truth, since I wasn't there to do it? Is that why you came here to kill me?" Clara hissed through the helm.

The queen's eyes widened in surprise.

"You want to know why?" she asked in a slimy voice, revealing the true nature of her ugly soul.

"No. I do not." Clara cut her short, "I care not to understand why the hateful hate. It isn't a problem within me that forces you to despise me. It is a problem within *you*."

The queen's mouth remained agape from shock and before she could respond Clara went on.

"You were never the loveliest of them all, your *highness*. Nor shall you be," she mocked, removing the helm from her head.

Her power was like drinking straight from a ray of sunshine. It was beautiful, and it burned a scorching heat that left only the best parts of you alive. Unfortunately for the queen, there were no best parts of her. She was all wretched.

Her flesh dried up and pressed to her bones as her muscles atrophied and decayed in front of our very eyes. The Ao Ao growled, scratching up at the tree as if it were a dog hunting for a bone until eventually, she breathed her last painful breath.

"Shall we get her down? Feed her to your pet?" I asked her.

"Yes please." She smiled a wicked grin before turning on her heels and skipping back through the path the same way we arrived.

Epilogue
-the warlock-

Three years later—

Life was different with Clara now. The trees themselves had spaced apart to make room for the sun to shine in the forest canopy. The birds sang and the beasts became domesticated under her love. She insisted she had never felt happier, freer, than here with us. But the truth was that she had actually freed us all.

It was impossible to not believe her. She wore that smile on her face that lit up the entire night sky and I had no choice but to return one of my own. Right now though, her expression was hidden, covered by the helm as she stalked towards me completely nude.

Each curve of her body begging to be squeezed, bitten, and licked by me. If I closed my eyes and thought hard enough I could remember how her pussy felt just this morning when I fucked her over the breakfast table.

But now I was tied up, arms behind my back and wrists bound together. She stood over my legs before lowering herself down into a squatted position. I exhaled heavily in anticipation, reaching my hips as high as I could in a silent plea for her to drop down on me.

She chuckled, an evil sound formed out of the helm, and my cock leaked a bead of precum. She finally lowered herself, dropping to her open knees with my legs between hers.

"Do it," I growled and she dropped her head back with a laugh.

"You are not the one in charge here, husband." It was meant to sound sweet but with the helm on it was anything but.

"Fuck me," I groaned out.

It was absolute torture watching her beautiful body dangle in front of me like a cherry ripe for the picking. I would never have my fill of her. It would never be enough. I would never be satisfied no matter how many lifetimes we lived together. She pulled the helm off and pressed her lips to mine as if she could read my mind and feel the pull of my emotions.

"I love you," she whispered before sinking down onto my cock.

We moaned in sync at the feeling of uniting our bodies again and she dropped her head back in bliss. I took her nipple in my mouth, and used my magic to make the bindings disappear.

I ached to touch her.

My fingers found her hardened clit slick with desire and I rubbed, giving her the friction she craved desperately with each bounce of her hips.

"I love you too," I whispered in her ear and she unraveled in my arms, convulsing through her climax while I continued to thrust.

I grabbed her waist and flipped her under me, grabbing each of her ankles and placing them on my shoulder to let me go deeper. She sobbed a hearty sound with each slam of my cock inside her, her pussy continuously spasming as if her climax had no start or end. She milked my cock until I could not hold it back any longer and my hot cum spilled inside her.

We laid on the floor, catching our breath, and I brought her to my chest. She was everything I did not know I had been waiting for.

And we had saved each other.

About the author

Santana Knox is the pen name of a Brazilian writer, neuro-divergent creative, follower of Santa Muerte and self acclaimed Witch who emerges from the foulest swamp bogs to bring you even filthier stories. Santana got tired of letting the voices in her head drive her crazy, and decided to write down the stories they were begging to tell instead. A lover of the unusual, and a hopeless romantic when it comes to toxic villains, Santana's books should always be taken with a grain of salt, specifically the kind that keeps demons away.

To enter her cult, join her facebook reading group: Santana's Psychos, like her on facebook, or follow her on social media. (@Santana.knox)

More books by Santana:

Heartless Heathens - A why choose gothic romance stand-alone

Reina del Cártel Series: Complete

Queen of Nothing (Book 1)

Reign of Ruin (Book 2)

Empire of Carnage (Book 3)

Diablos Locos Motorcycle Club

No Place for Devils (book 1)

Made in the USA
Monee, IL
11 January 2025